SNOW WHITE
and ROSE RED

SNOW WHITE and ROSE RED

STORY BY THE BROTHERS GRIMM

Pictures by BARBARA COONEY

Delacorte
Press

For Gretel and Phoebe

Published by
Delacorte Press
Bantam Doubleday Dell Publishing Group, Inc.
666 Fifth Avenue
New York, New York 10103

This work was first published in Great Britain by
Constable Young Books Ltd., London.

Library of Congress Cataloging in Publication Data
Cooney, Barbara, [date of birth] Snow-White and Rose-Red :
a picture book / by Barbara Cooney.   p.   cm.
    Retelling of Schneeweisschen und Rosenrot, originally by the brothers Grimm.
    Summary: A bear, befriended by two sisters during the winter, returns one day
to reward them royally for their kindness.
    ISBN 0-385-30175-8. — ISBN 0-385-30176-6 (lib. bdg.)
    [1. Fairy tales. 2. Folklore—Germany.] I. Schneeweisschen und Rosenrot.
English. II. Title.   PZ8.C7888Sn 1990   398.2—dc20
[E]   89-78013   CIP   AC
Manufactured in the United States of America
One Previous Edition
February 1991
10 9 8 7 6 5 4 3 2 1

poor widow once lived with her two children in a lonely little cottage. In the garden grew two rosebushes, one red and the other white, and because the children were like the roses that grew on the bushes, one was named Snow White and the other Rose Red.

They were as good children as ever lived, always busy and cheerful. Rose Red loved to run about in the meadows looking for flowers and butterflies, while Snow White, who was quiet and gentle, preferred to stay at home helping her mother or reading to her if there was nothing else to do.

The children loved each other so dearly that, whenever they went out, they walked hand in hand, and whatever one girl had was always divided with the other.

Often they went into the woods to gather berries, but no harm ever came to them. The little hare ate cabbage leaves from their hands; the deer grazed by their side; and the birds sat on the branches nearby and sang to them.

If night came on before they left the woods, they lay down on the moss and slept till morning. And because their mother knew they would do so, she did not worry about them.

Snow White and Rose Red kept their mother's cottage so clean that it was a pleasure to look at it. Every morning in the summertime, Rose Red swept the kitchen and placed a fresh bouquet of roses by her mother's bedside before she was up.

Every morning in the winter Snow White made the fire and put the kettle on to boil. Although made of copper, the kettle shone like gold, so well did little Snow White keep it polished.

In the evenings when the snow fell, the mother would say, "Go and bolt the door, Snow White." Then they would all sit down by the fire, and the mother would put on her spectacles and read from a large book while the two girls listened and spun. Near them on the floor lay a little lamb, while perched in one corner sat a white dove with its head under its wing.

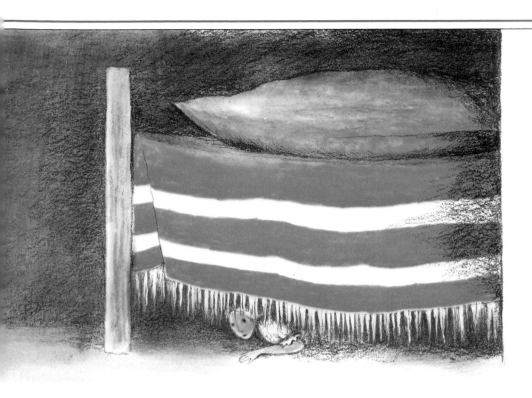

One evening as they were sitting together, there was an urgent knock on the door.

"Quick, Rose Red," said the mother, "open the door; it may be some traveler who is looking for shelter."

Rose Red opened the door, thinking there was some poor man outside. But instead a huge black bear poked his head inside. Rose Red screamed loudly and jumped back; the lamb gave a frightened bleat; the dove flew wildly around the room; and little Snow White hid under her mother's bed.

The bear, however, began to talk and said, "Don't be afraid, I won't hurt you. I am half frozen and only wish to warm myself by your fire."

"You poor bear!" said the mother. "Come in and lie down by the fire, but take care that you do not burn your fur." Then she called, "Snow White, Rose Red, come here. The bear will not hurt you."

The children came out; the lamb did the same; and finally even the dove stopped fluttering. Then the bear said, "Get the broom, children, and brush the snow from my fur." So they brought the broom and brushed him clean. Then, growling cheerfully, he stretched himself out comfortably before the fire.

In a short time the children became friendly enough to tease and play with their clumsy guest. They tugged at his shaggy fur, planted their feet against his back, pushed him first one way and then another, and even hit him with a hazel twig. Now and then he pretended to grumble and made the girls laugh.

When it was bedtime, and the children were in bed, the mother said to the bear, "You may lie by the hearth all night if you want to. You will at least be protected from the cold and bad weather."

As soon as morning dawned, the children let him out, and he trotted away over the snow to the woods. But every evening afterward, he came back at a certain hour to the cottage, lay down at the hearth, and allowed the children to play with him for a little while. They became so accustomed to his visits that the door was never bolted until their black friend had arrived.

One day in spring, when everything was green, he said to Snow White, "I must go away now, and I shall not return during the whole summer."

Snow White felt very sorry to part with the bear. As she sadly opened the door for him to leave, his fur caught on the latch and tore. Snow White thought she saw something glitter like gold under his fur, but she was not sure, for the bear trotted hastily away and was soon lost to sight among the trees.

Some time after this, the mother sent the children into the woods to gather sticks for the fire. As they approached the forest, they came to a large tree that was lying across the path, and something was hopping up and down beside it. They could not imagine what it was. When they came nearer, they saw a little dwarf with a wrinkled face and a

snowy-white beard a yard long. The end of his beard had caught in a cleft in the tree, and the little man jumped about like a dog on a chain, not knowing how to free himself.

He glared at the girls with his fiery eyes and cried, "Why do you just stand there? Can't you come and help me?"

"What have you done, little man?" asked Rose Red.

"You foolish goose!" he cried. "I was trying to split the tree to get a little wood for our kitchen. I had driven in the wedge, and everything was going well, when suddenly it flew out, and the tree closed up so quickly that my beautiful white beard was caught, and I cannot get it out. Don't just stand there and laugh, you silly milk-faced creatures!"

The children tried as hard as they could to get his beard out, but it was caught too fast. Finally one of them said, "I will run and get someone to help us."

"Stupid blockheads!" snarled the dwarf. "Who wants any more people? You are two too many for me now. Can't you think of anything better?"

"Don't be impatient," said Snow White. "I can help you." And taking her scissors from her pocket, she cut off the end of his beard.

As soon as the dwarf felt himself free, he snatched up a sack full of gold that he had hidden among the roots of the tree, and throwing it over his shoulder he stomped off, growling to himself, "Stupid people! They have cut off a piece of my beautiful beard. A plague on them." Then away he went without once giving the children a glance.

One day Snow White and Rose Red went fishing. As they got near the brook, they saw something hopping on the bank like a large grasshopper about to jump into the water. They ran toward it and saw it was the dwarf.

"What are you doing?" asked Rose Red. "You will fall into the water."

"I am not such a fool as to wish to do that!" he cried. "Don't you see that this fish is trying to pull me in?"

The little man had been sitting on the bank fishing. When a large fish swallowed his bait, his beard had become entangled in the line and he did not have the strength to draw it out. Instead, the fish began to pull him into the water. He had clung to the rushes and grass, but it was no use. He was fighting a losing battle.

The girls came just in the nick of time. Even so, at first their efforts were useless—beard and string were in a hopeless tangle. There was nothing to be done but to take out the scissors again and cut off another little piece of the beautiful beard.

The dwarf was in a great rage. "You toadstools!" he cried. "Do you want to disfigure my face? It was not enough that you cut it once, now you must take away the best part of it. I dare not show myself among my own people again. I wish you may have to run the soles off your boots before I see you again!"

Then he picked up a bag of pearls from the rushes and without another word disappeared behind a rock.

It happened soon after that the mother sent both girls to the village to buy needles and pins, thread and ribbons. As they walked along through a meadow, on which, here and

there, great stones lay scattered, they saw a large bird slowly
flying in a circle over their heads. It drew nearer and nearer
the earth till finally it sank down by one of the stones.

At the same instant they heard a piercing scream, and running toward the bird, they saw that their old friend the dwarf had been seized by the bird and was about to be carried off. The kind-hearted children at once grabbed hold of him and struggled with the eagle until he finally let go of his prize. As soon as the dwarf had recovered from his fright, he exclaimed in his shrill voice, "Could you not have treated me a little more politely? You have pulled on my fine coat so hard that it is all torn and full of holes. Clumsy meddlers, that's what you are!" Without a word of thanks, he picked up a bag of rubies and slipped into his den under the stone. The girls, who by now were used to his ingratitude, thought nothing of it but walked on to the village to do their errands.

On their way home, as they were crossing the meadow, they suddenly came upon the dwarf who, supposing that no one would pass at that late hour, had come out of his den so that he might spread out his jewels and admire them. They glittered and shone in the setting sun, and the children stopped to gaze at the wonderful sight.

"What are you standing there gaping at?" he cried, and his face became crimson with rage. He was still scolding the girls when a loud growling was heard and a great black bear lumbered out of the woods. The dwarf jumped up in fright, but he could not reach his den before the bear overtook him.

Then, terror stricken, he cried, "Dear bear, spare me! I will give you back all the treasures. See, there are the precious stones! Spare my life! Of what use would such a poor little fellow be to you? You would hardly feel me between your teeth. Here, take those two wicked girls. They will make nice tender morsels. They're as fat as young quails. Eat them instead of me!"

But the bear paid no attention to his words. He gave the dwarf just one blow with his great paw, and that was the end of the dwarf.

The girls were about to run away, but the bear called out, "Snow White, Rose Red, don't be afraid of me. Wait and I will go with you."

They knew his voice and stopped, but when the bear came up to them, his bearskin fell off and before them stood a tall and beautiful man, dressed entirely in gold.

"I am a king's son," he said. "The wicked dwarf bewitched me, stole all my treasures, and made me wander about in this forest in the form of a bear. Only his death could set me free."

Not many years afterward, Snow White was married to the Prince, and Rose Red to his brother, and all the treasure the dwarf had collected and hidden in his den was divided between them.

The old mother came to live with her daughters. The rosebushes were also brought to the castle and planted in front of it. And every year they bore beautiful red and white roses.

Other books illustrated by Barbara Cooney:

Chanticleer and the Fox
Island Boy
The Little Juggler
Miss Rumphius
Ox-Cart Man
Squawk to the Moon
The Story of Holly and Ivy

Barbara Cooney has illustrated more than one hundred books for children. Among her numerous awards are two Caldecotts, for *Chanticleer and the Fox* and *Ox-Cart Man,* and the American Book Award for *Miss Rumphius.* She lives in Damariscotta, Maine.